Mr. Mosquito Put on His Tuxedo

by BARBARA OLENYIK MORROW

illustrated by PONDER GOEMBEL

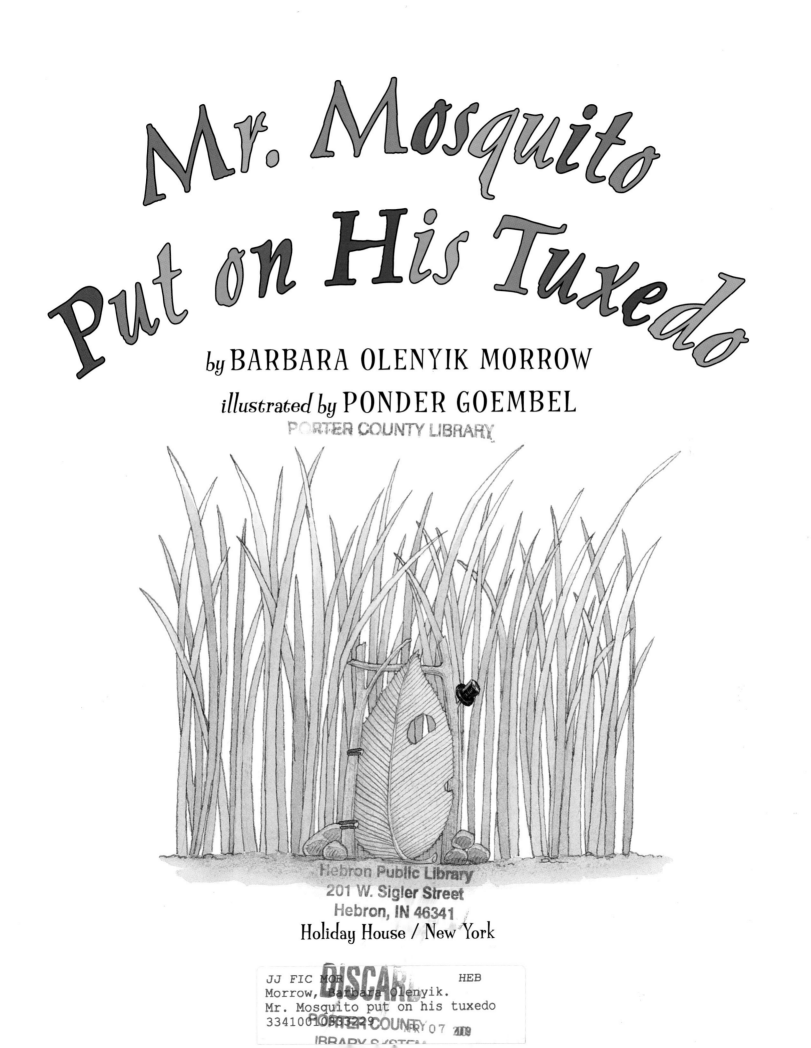

Holiday House / New York

To Miss Deb the Librarian, and to Julia, Mindy, Kathy,
Sandie, Elizabeth, Crystal, and Natalie, writing coaches all
—B. O. M.

In memory of Edward Gorey
—P. G.

Text copyright © 2009 by Barbara Olenyik Morrow
Illustrations copyright © 2009 by Ponder Goembel
All Rights Reserved
Printed and Bound in China
The text typeface is Pink Martini.
The illustrations were done in colored ink line with acrylic wash.
www.holidayhouse.com
First Edition
1 3 5 7 9 10 8 6 4 2

Library of Congress Cataloging-in-Publication Data
Morrow, Barbara Olenyik.
Mr. Mosquito put on his tuxedo / by Barbara Olenyik Morrow :
illustrated by Ponder Goembel. – 1st ed.
p. cm.
Summary: Mr. Mosquito saves the insect ball from an intruding bear.
ISBN-13: 978-0-8234-2072-8 (hardcover)
[1. Mosquitoes–Fiction. 2. Insects–Fiction. 3. Balls (Parties)–Fiction.
4. Stories in rhyme.] I. Goembel, Ponder, ill. II. Title.
PZ8.3.M8365Mr 2009
[E]–dc22
2007025486

Mr. Mosquito put on his tuxedo.

He flew out the door to the ball.

He waved to Ms. Spider but couldn't invite her.

"So sorry—just insects, that's all."

Mr. Mosquito arrived a bit tardy.
The doormen were Horsefly and Gnat.
They shooed him right in:
"Where on earth have you been?"
"My limousine—drat!—had a flat."

Mr. Mosquito strolled down a red carpet.
He bowed to his host, the Queen Bee.
"Your Highness," he said,
"you are looking well fed.
I saw your hive—LIVE—on TV."

Mr. Mosquito glanced round for a partner.
He waltzed with a wasp and they twirled.
"I daresay your stinger is quite a humdinger."
Wasp whispered, "It's out of this world."

Mr. Mosquito rushed up to a cockroach.
"Dear chap, could you bring me some punch?
And a pint would be nice—
of chilled blood over ice.
I've not had a bite since my lunch."

Mr. Mosquito bumped into some bedbugs.
He gushed, "*Mes petites! You've been missed!*"
"We went pillow shopping,"
they cooed without stopping.
They all exchanged bug-hugs and kissed.

When suddenly . . .

from off in the distance arose a great racket.
GASP! Louder and louder it grew.
All the ladybugs shrieked. Fifty fireflies freaked.
A cricket collapsed and turned blue.

"How ghastly!" "How awful!" "How frightful!" "How horrid!"
cried moths as they peeked out the door.
Then the ground—how it shook!
No one else dared to look.
All dreaded what might be in store.

"Speak up! Someone save us!"
six beetles all bellowed.
"Speak up!" sobbed cicadas off-key.
Mr. Mosquito, swift as a torpedo,
said, "Please. I insist. Allow me."

He sped from the ballroom and ventured forth boldly.
The night air was heavy with heat.
He looked to his right, where the moonlight shone bright.
He spied—*eeeeeegad!!!*—BIG FEET!

Onward and onward, yes, BIG FEET kept coming.
Tromp-tromping! Crunch-crunching! Oh my!
Mr. Mosquito zoomed round incognito.
He had to act quickly—or die.

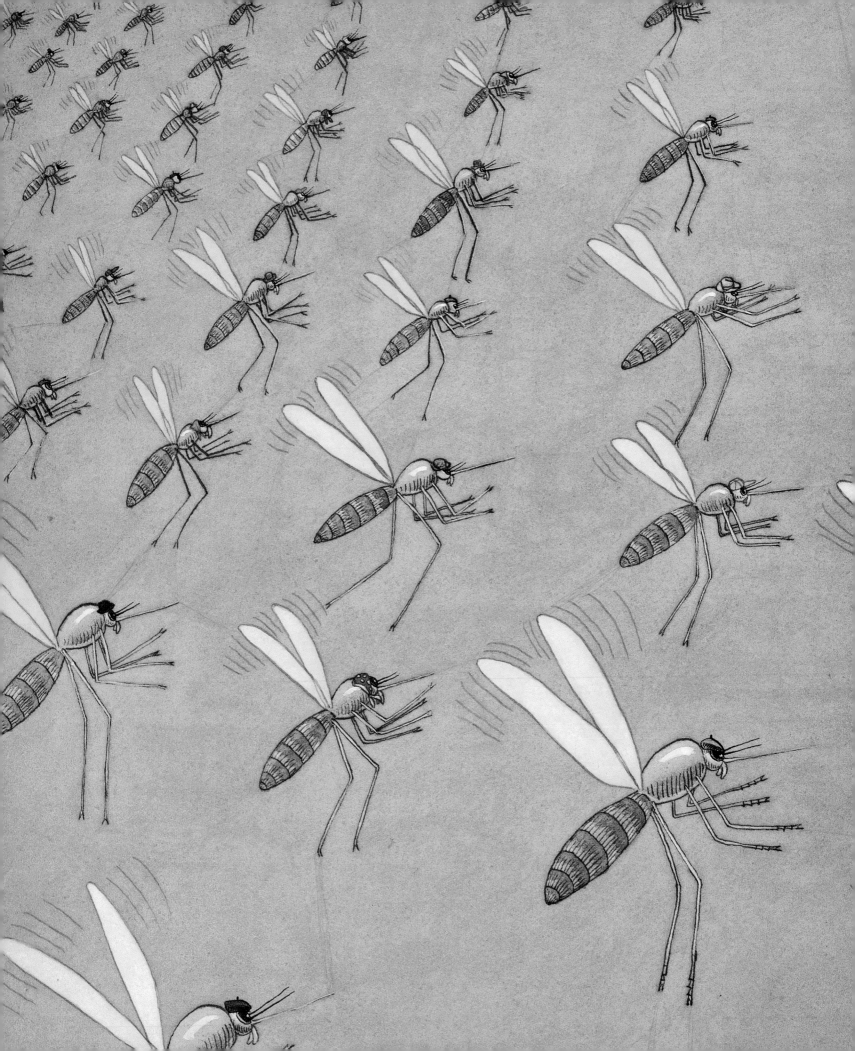

He sent out a signal and summoned his kinfolk.
His cousins and uncles and aunts.
From swamp and from wood
came mosquitoes that could.
Some traveled from faraway France.

Mr. Mosquito instructed with passion:
"Prepare! Point antennae! Deploy!
We swarm out tonight
to drive BIG FEET from sight.
Are you ready? Get set. Go annoy!!!!"

Bzzz, bzzz, bzzz, bzzz, bzzz, bzzz, bzzz, bzzz, bzzz, bzzz! Bzzz!

"Mission accomplished!" crowed Mr. Mosquito,
adjusting his coattails and tie.
He thanked all his kin. He heard music begin.
He rejoined the ball by and by.

"Our party! You saved it!" The locusts cheered loudly.
"Our hero! Mosquito! Hooray!"
"'Twas nothing," he said, his wings turning bright red.
"I like to annoy. It's like play."

Mr. Mosquito was hoisted and carried.
An army of ants raised him high.
Termites saluted, and dragonflies rooted.
"All hail him!" sang one butterfly.

Mr. Mosquito was led to Her Highness.
"Young man," she decreed, "you're the best!
For acting so gallant and sharing your talent,
I dub you my . . .

Royal . . .